FRANKENSTEIN

FRANKENSTEIN

The Modern Prometheus

Adapted From The Novel By Mary Shelley

Martin Powell • Writer

Patrick Olliffe • Artist

Patrick Olliffe • Cover

Clem Robins • Letterer

Dave Olbrich • Publisher

Chris Ulm • Editor-In-Chief

Mickie Villa • Associate Editor

Dan Danko • Editorial Assistant

Tom Mason • Creative Director

Dinosaurs For Hire: Guns 'N Lizards
At last, a sensitive tale of teen-age angst and the trauma of growing up in middle class America. Just kidding! It's really about Dinosaurs with automatic weapons. By Tom Mason. Illustrated by Bryon Carson and Mike Roberts.

The Three Stooges: The Knuckleheads Return
Nyuk! Nyuk! Nyuk! These knuckleheads are back in a collection of seven slapstick adventures! Edited by Tom Mason.

Abbot And Costello: The Classic Comics
Bud Abbot and Lou Costello are reunited in this collection of 20 classic comic stories from their heyday. Edited by Tom Mason.

Spicy Detective Stories
A classic collection of seven two-fisted 1930's pulp detective stories from the pages of Spicy Detective magazine. Edited By Tom Mason.

Tiger-X: The Adventure Begins
Only one thing can free the United States from Soviet domination--the secret weapon known only as Tiger-X! By Ninja High School creator Ben Dunn.

China Sea
An epic adventure in the tradition of Terry And The Pirates. By Barry Blair.

The Trouble With Girls
Lester Girls would like nothing more than to curl up with a good book in a quiet, suburban bungalow. Instead, he's stuck with a ceaseless round of luscious babes, high adventure, uncountable riches, and break-neck action. By Will Jacobs and Gerard Jones. Illustrated by Tim Hamilton and Dave Garcia.

The Trouble With Girls Volume Two: My Name Is Girls
Adventurer, hero, tycoon, lover...Lester Girls is all of this and more. Yet, he is not a happy man. All he wants are t simple things in life--a mousy wife, a routine job, and a pair of sensible shoes. For Lester Girls, the simplest thing are the hardest to attain! By Will Jacobs and Gerard Jones. Illustrated by Tim Hamilton.

Scimidar Book One: Pleasure And Pain
She's a poet, a lover, a dreamer. She's also a sexy, empathic tracker in the year 2005. Absorbing the emotions o those around her, she is a walking time bomb. She is Scimidar. By R.A. Jones. Illustrated by Rob Davis with Alber Val and James Baldwin. Mature subject matter. Not intended for children.

Scarlet In Gaslight
Sherlock Holmes meets Dracula in the strangest case of his career! By Martin Powell and Seppo Makinen.

Dark Wolf
Priest by day, vengeful killer by night. By R.A. Jones and Butch Burcham.

Plan Nine From Outer Space
John Wooley adapts the "Worst Movie Ever Made." Illustrated by Stan Timmons and Bruce McCordindale.

FRANKENSTEIN
Graphic Album
Published by Malibu Graphics, Inc. 1355 Lawrence Dr. #212
Newbury Park, CA 91320. 805/499-3015. Printed in the USA
First Printing. ISBN# 0-944735-39-8 $9.95 • $11.95 In Canada

741.5
P885f

089222

Of Men And Monsters

Introduction by Ron Fortier

In 1818, a brilliant young woman named Mary Wollstonecraft Shelley wrote a graphic novel entitled *The Modern Prometheus*. It is the tale of a young Swiss doctor who attempts to play God without fully comprehending the consequence of so exalted position. In the end the creation of his arrogance destroys him both physically and spiritually. The story of Victor Frankenstein and his monster is truly one of the finest horror melodramas ever penned.

But wait, you already know that, don't you? As a classic of English literature, Mary Shelley's *Frankenstein* (as it later became known) has been reprinted and replayed in the various media more times than any army of historians could ever properly document. Is there a single movie buff in existence who has not seen and subsequently been moved by the late Boris Karloff's inspired portrayal of the monster in the 1931 Universal Picture? It seems highly unlikely.

And the comics! Our patch-work Adam has been the focus of countless graphic interpretations from the original Classics Illustrated to Berni Wrightson's stunning pieces for the Marvel edition of a few years back. Somehow, Mary Shelley tapped a universal chord in all of us that continually draws us to this stark and tragic narrative again and again.

Still the pragmatic side to our nature must cry enough! Why in the blue blazes would anyone want to do another *Frankenstein*?

In the pages that follow, you will learn the answer to that question most poignantly. Prepare yourself for a sumptuous reading feast for both the eye and the intellect.

Martin Powell is a poet who writes prose. Sound simple? Hardly. Only one other writer has ever been able to pull off that particular trick, and his name is Ray Bradbury. Powell's words are elegant and seductive. They come at you with a soft whisper that only goes away hours after you've read them. He lures you into characters so human, so perfect, the borders between fictional and reality blur, sweeping the reader into the thick of it. If you are truly brave, same this volume for a dark stormy night when you are all alone in the house. Sit by a single lamp and enter Powell's world of moving shadows. Soon your palms will begin to sweat and your ears will hear strange sounds coming from empty rooms.

Enter Patrick Olliffe. Where Powell assaults your sensibilities with his deadly subtleness, Olliffe delivers the killing blow with the most graceful graphic art ever produced in the history of this genre. His masterful use of the black and white conflict pounds at the viewer with continued force. In Olliffe's hands the beautiful and the ugly meet, they embrace and dance the wonderous danse macabre.

With the finishing flourishes of Clem Robins truly vital lettering that achieves its purpose without once ever diminishing the art and Chris Ulm's deft editing hand, we realize at last our answer to our initial query.

Why on Earth do another *Frankenstein*?

Because my friends, it has never been done correctly.

Until now.

Ron Fortier
November 1989

The Monster
Introduction by Patrick Olliffe

F *rankenstein* had been one of "those" projects for me. A book I had wanted to do, but could not see happening anytime in the near future. Fortunately, for me, Eternity comics gave Martin Powell and I the opportunity to create what I hope will be viewed as one of the best comic adaptations of Mary Shelley's novel.

We discussed the direction in which Martin wanted to take the book, and from this conversation I arrived at the basic concept of how I wanted the book to look. What if someone had *really* undertaken the task of creating a human life, I wondered. The end result would look as close to an actual human as could be achieved using dissected cadavers and the raw materials available during that time period—no flat head or bolts in the neck. This creature, although disfigured, scarred and awkward, would still resemble that

from which he was made.

It was from both my own imagination and Shelley's original descriptions that I created "my" monster. Hopefully, the end results enhanced Martin's powerful script and aided in the emotional impact that we wanted this book to have on those who experience it.

—**Patrick Olliffe**
December 1989

Phantoms, Forests and Gum Cards

Forword by Martin Powell

W hen I was a boy, visiting relatives in the country, I often sat in the dewy night grass and stared at the blackened woods, wondering what nameless monsters lurked and haunted behind the tangles of ivy and oak. My brothers (and several imaginative cousins) were always quick to impress such fanciful phantoms upon my youthful gullibility. Even so, I always forgave them and was always eager to hear more, collecting each spook story like other boys accumulated gum cards. I guess everyone has thrilled, at one time or another, to a ghost story, relishing a sense of ghoulish wonder at what really *may* be awaiting us in those darkened woods.

Mary Shelley certaily did.

Reaching back into her fertile, teen-aged brain, Mary—wife of the English poet Percy Shelley—created a gothic masterpiece in *Frankenstein or the Modern Prometheus*, the greatest and most influential horror story ever written, and the basis for this three-issue limited-series.

After the swift success of my Sherlock Holmes/Dracula series, *Scarlet in Gaslight*, Eternity Comics was willing to give me another project, especially indicating they were interested in material of a similar nature. My next Holmes series, *A Case of Blind Fear*, was already in the works and, hesitating to use Count Dracula again so soon, the *Frankenstein* concept appealed to me the most. It didn't take long for me to work up a series proposal, and it's more to Mary Shelley's credit than to mine that the submission sold immediately. The powerful story had haunted me for years, becoming a dream-project, long conceived and repressed, and now it was in my grasp. But how would I approach such a retelling of so time-honored a classic?

I had decided early to tell the tale of the book itself. It's Mary's story, although I haven't exactly ignored the cinematic sources, and others, that have added to and embellished the original myth over the last hundred and seventy years. Lovers of the novel will find themselves among old friends, while new readers will meet some of the most compelling characters in English literature outside the works of Shakespeare.

This retelling owes a tremendous debt to Patrick Olliffe's wonderfully moody and enigmatic illustrations; Pat establishes a tangible atmosphere within a single panel, and we happily agreed early on to the same dark, grim and passionate vision for Mary's story. He's been the ideal work-mate and his inspired version is, so I believe, the definitive *Frankenstein* in comics.

Also, I acknowledge special thanks to my editor Chris Ulm, who helped give the opening sequence an added punch, and to Forest J. Ackerman; without his classic Famous Monsters of Filmland magazine I may never have discovered the Frankenstein Monster at all.

It is to Mr. Ackerman and to the gentle ghost of Boris Karloff that this series is affectionately dedicated.

—Martin Powell
December, 1989

THE FIEND.

IT WON'T BE LONG NOW-- THERE'S NO ESCAPE.

FIRST TO FORTIFY MYSELF,

I MUST BE STRONG...

FOR REVENGE'S SAKE,

WHIMPER

BUT I SHAN'T FORGET *YOU*, MY FRIENDS.

IT IS TOO LATE FOR ME--IT IS *YOUR* STRENGTH WHICH WILL DELIVER HIM TO ME.

DEATH TO THE MONSTER!

FOR ELIZABETH...

YOU!!

FRANKENSTEIN

FROM THE NOVEL BY MARY WOLLSTONECRAFT SHELLEY
BOOK ONE : "THE MODERN PROMETHEUS"

WRITTEN BY
MARTIN POWELL

ILLUSTRATED BY
PATRICK OLLIFFE

LETTERED BY
CLEM ROBINS

EDITED BY
CHRIS ULM

ELIZABETH --PLEASE!

I HAVE AN EXAMINATION TOMORROW...

≩GIGGLE≩

I'M SORRY, VICTOR. CAN I HELP?

NO, ELIZABETH, I...I SHOULDN'T HAVE BEEN CROSS WITH YOU. I'LL PLAY A GAME LATER--I PROMISE. THAT'S FAIR, ISN'T IT?

I THINK NOT!

HAHAHAHA

WHA--!

NOW YOU'VE DONE IT!

⑦

ELIZABETH!!

HERE NOW, SIR. STEADY YOURSELF. YOU'VE HAD A *NIGHTMARE*, THAT'S ALL.

NIGHTMARE?

CAN IT BE?

YOU'RE QUITE SAFE NOW, WE ALL HAVE BAD DREAMS.

NO... NO!

IT WASN'T A DREAM! IT WASN'T...

THE MONSTER REAL--!

THE MONSTER...

YES--JUST QUIET DOWN. THAT'S IT. I AM ROBERT WALTON, CAPTAIN OF THIS ENGLISH EXPLOR-ATION VESSEL. YOU HAVE BEEN VERY ILL...

YOU-- THINK I AM MAD?

SADLY, IT IS NOT SO.

BELIEVE ME, CAPTAIN, MY PLIGHT IS GENUINE AND MY SUFFERING EXTENDS BEYOND THE FLESH. FOR THE *SAFETY* OF THIS SHIP --AND OF ITS CREW--PER-HAPS I SHOULD TELL THE TALE...

YES.

SOMEHOW, TONIGHT I FEEL I *MUST*.

9

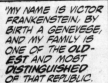

"MY NAME IS VICTOR FRANKENSTEIN, BY BIRTH A GENEVESE, AND MY FAMILY IS ONE OF THE **OLDEST** AND MOST **DISTINGUISHED** OF THAT REPUBLIC."

"BEFORE THE DEATH OF MY MOTHER, MY LIFE WAS UNREMARKABLE, NO ONE COULD HAVE PASSED A HAPPIER CHILDHOOD THAN I."

"THROUGH MY FATHER'S INFLUENCE, I ATTENDED THE UNIVERSITY OF INGOLSTADT TO STUDY MEDICINE WITH THE UPPER CLASSMEN."

"MIND YOU, IT WASN'T THE ART OF **HEALING** THAT DROVE ME..."

"...THE STRUCTURE OF THE HUMAN FRAME BEING MY CHIEF FASCINATION."

YOU MUST CONCERN YOURSELF WITH **LIFE**, HERR FRANKENSTEIN-- NOT **DEATH** AND **DECAY**...

"ITS STRENGTHS AND WEAKNESSES.

"ITS **MORTALITY**."

"SOMEWHERE, AMONG THE VAULTS AND GALLOWS, WAS THE ANSWER TO THIS GREATEST OF MYSTERIES."

"TO KNOW THE SECRETS OF LIFE, I PROBED THE CAUSE AND PROGRESS OF **DECOMPOSITION**.

"SEARCHING.

"RESEARCHING."

"IT WAS THE RIDDLE OF **LIFE** ITSELF I SOUGHT. IT BECAME MY **OBSESSION**.

"UNTIL SUDDENLY, IN THE MIDST OF MY DARKNESS, A LIGHT **BURST** UPON ME...

"THUS, THROUGH FEVERED LABOUR AND FATIGUE, I HAD DISCOVERED THE FORMULA OF GENERATING **LIFE**.

"AND MORE, **I MYSELF** BECAME CAPABLE OF BESTOWING ANIMATION UPON LIFELESS TISSUE."

I--I DIDN'T DO IT... I SWEAR!

PLEASE LEAVE ME ALONE!

"...SO WONDEROUSLY BRILLIANT-- YET SO SIMPLE--THAT I BECAME DIZZY WITH ITS **AWESOME** POSSIBILITIES."

"THE DREAM."

BLAM!

A GUNSHOT--?

"RACING WITH DECAY AND FIGHTING AGAINST FAILURE, I SHAMEFULLY CONFESS I SELDOM SPARED THOUGHT FOR *HOME*...

"...OF MY FATHER AND BROTHER.

"OF ELIZABETH.

"IT WAS LIKE *THE DEVIL* HIMSELF GUIDED MY PLANS.

"HANGINGS AND MOB VIOLENCE RENDERED MY WORK.

"FROM FILTHY DISEASE AND STREET MURDER I WOVE MY *MIRACLE.*"

REST WHILE YOU MAY, OLD MAN.

YOU'RE GOING TO A *BETTER* LIFE.

15

"IN MY FEVERED BRAIN I IMAGINED MYSELF A MODERN ACOLYTE OF THE GREAT PROMETHEUS...

"...MOLDING THE FORM OF MAN FROM THE DUST OF THE GRAVE...

"NEITHER EATING NOR SLEEPING...

"...UNTIL THE FIRES OF HEAVEN OBEYED ME."

ON A STORMY NIGHT IN NOVEMBER CAME THE TERRIBLE CLIMAX.

"THE *THING* BREATHED HARD..."

"A CONVULSIVE MOTION AGITATED ITS LIMBS..."

HIS FACE...

MY DEAR GOD.

19

NO--NO! GET AWAY!

DON'T TOUCH ME!

"FLIGHT WAS MY ONLY RECOURSE.

I RACED BLINDLY INTO THE NIGHT, DIMLY AWARE OF THE WET THRASHING BEHIND ME.

"MY MIND REELED WITH THE HORROR I HAD DONE. I HAD SEEN ITS UGLINESS FOR MONTHS...

"...BUT TO OBSERVE LIFE IN THE YELLOW EYES, EXPRESSION ON THE DISTORTED FACE...

"...AND TO WATCH IT LUMBER TOWARD ME..."

BACK! GET BACK!

DON'T TOUCH ME--!

PLEASE...

VICTOR?

WHAT ON EARTH--?

21

VICTOR!

AAH! AAH...
AAH...

OH GOD.

IT'S ALL
RIGHT,
VICTOR.
I'M HERE.

HENRY?
IS THAT...

...YOU?

23

IT IS INDEED, MY POOR FRIEND. THE BRAIN FEVER HAS PASSED--YOU'VE BEEN UNDER ITS SPELL FOR NEARLY *THREE MONTHS.*

MONTHS...? HENRY--MY FAMILY... *ELIZABETH...*

...AND HE SAYS HE FEELS STRONGER EVERY DAY, AND BEGS OUR FORGIVENESS OF HIS LONG SILENCE. HENRY CONTINUES TO NURSE HIM, SPEEDING HIS RECOVERY.

THEY ARE WELL, AND CONCERNED ABOUT YOU. I'VE BEEN SENDING THEM REGULAR MESSAGES OF YOUR PROGRESS, THOUGH, IN TRUTH, THEY DON'T REALIZE HOW VERY ILL YOU'VE BEEN. A LETTER IN YOUR OWN HAND WILL SET THEIR MINDS AT EASE, VICTOR.

YOUNG CLERVAL IS A GOOD LAD. DO YOU WISH TO GO TO VICTOR, CHILD?

OH, UNCLE ALPHONSE! THERE IS NO NEED! HE PROMISES A LONG VISIT DURING THE EASTER HOLIDAYS!

AH, THERE YOU ARE, WILLIAM. I'VE A *SURPRISE* FOR YOU--YOUR *BROTHER* IS COMING HOME NEXT MONTH!

REALLY? VICTOR'S COMING! WILL HE BRING ME A PRESENT?!

HAVING VICTOR WE[LL] AND SAFE[IS] GIFT ENO[UGH] WILLY.

YOU SHOULD HAVE GONE WITH THEM CHILD. IT'S SUCH A LOVELY DAY FOR A PICNIC, ESPECIALLY NOW.

NOT TODAY, DEAR UNCLE--I MUST ANSWER THIS STRAIGHT AWAY...

MY *LOVE* IS COMING HOME!

25

YOU ARE BEGINNING TO LOOK *YOURSELF* AGAIN, VICTOR.

BECAUSE OF YOUR CARE, HENRY. HOW CAN I *EVER* REPAY THE DEBT?

IT'S GOOD TO BE GOING HOME, FINALLY.

EH? WHAT'S THIS? A SPECIAL DELIVERY LETTER?

HA, HA! NONSENSE, MY FRIEND. COME ALONG NOW. I'LL HELP YOU PACK. REMEMBER YOU'RE LEAVING WITHIN THE WEEK.

HENRY...DEAR GOD! WILLIAM IS DEAD! *MURDERED!*

BUT, HOW CAN THIS BE? WHO COULD'VE--

FATHER SAYS THEY HAVE ARRESTED JUSTINE MORITZ ...ON *IRON-CLAD* EVIDENCE.

"I RACED HOME TO GENEVA. I WAS TOO LATE."

I CAN'T BELIEVE IT! YOU MUST SPEED YOUR DEPARTURE, OLD FRIEND. YOUR FAMILY *NEEDS* YOU.

"THE TRIAL WAS OVER."

PITY, YOUNG GIRL LIKE THAT. PRETTY ONE, TOO.

DID SHE CONFESS?

NO NEED. A PRICELESS LOCKET BELONGING TO THE FRANKENSTEIN CHILD WAS FOUND ON HER. NEVER TRUST A *GOVERNESS*, I ALWAYS SAY...

VICTOR--?!

I'M *SORRY*, ELIZABETH...SO SORRY. I'VE BEEN AWAY TOO LONG.

SHE WAS INNOCENT, VICTOR--I *KNOW* SHE WAS.

YOUR FATHER IS A BROKEN MAN... HE DIDN'T EVEN COME TO COURT.

PLEASE GO HOME TO HIM. TELL HIM I'VE ARRIVED AND WILL BE THERE DIRECTLY.

"ELIZABETH'S BEAUTY HAD GROWN PALE AND THIN DURING MY TIME AWAY FROM HER. LITTLE WILLIAM HAD BEEN LIKE HER OWN CHILD SINCE MOTHER HAD DIED.

"THE GUILT OF MY LONG ABSENCE BORE HEAVILY UPON ME AS I SAW INTO HER BREAKING HEART.

"IF ONLY I'D BEEN THERE FOR HER, AND FOR FATHER.

"FOR WILLIAM.

27

"I HAD FAILED THEM ALL.

"THE SUN HAD SET UPON THE GALLOWS, AND I DID NOT LEAVE. TO IMAGINE THE PAIN IN MY FATHER'S EYES WAS *UNBEARABLE*.

"I WANDERED AIMLESSLY THROUGH THE CEMETERY, GRATEFUL FOR A MOMENT OF SOLITUDE, NEVER THINKING, EVEN FOR A MOMENT...

SNAP

"...THAT I WAS NOT ALONE."

"ALWAYS I SEE THE HORRID FACE BEFORE ME--EVEN ASLEEP THE COLOURLESS, LOATHING EYES NEVER LEAVE ME...

"..HELLISH FEATURES THAT I ALONE CONSTRUCTED."

MASTER.

FROM THE NOVEL BY MARY WOLLSTONECRAFT SHELLEY

BOOK TWO "THE MONSTER"

Written by **MARTIN POWELL** Illustrated by **PATRICK OLLIFFE** Letterer **CLEM ROBINS** Edited by **CHRIS ULM**

ENTER AND *WARM* YOURSELF, VICTOR FRANKENSTEIN.

I AM HERE AND I AM LISTENING. BUT I MUST KNOW...WAS IT YOU WHO KILLED MY BROTHER, WILLIAM?

CONFESS THE DEED! *ADMIT IT!* I *MUST* KNOW!

AT LEAST, I MAY RELIEVE YOU OF THAT MYSTERY ...THOUGH FOR MYSELF THERE IS NO COMFORT IN THE TRUTH.

I AM *GUILTY*... THE DESTROYER OF THE PURE AND THE INNOCENT. I WILL BE FOREVER HAUNTED BY THE TRUSTING BLOOD ON MY HANDS. YOU HAVE CREATED AN ABOMINATION, FRANKENSTEIN--A CREATURE WITH NO PLACE IN THIS WORLD OR ANY OTHER.

STAY YOUR HATRED, CREATOR, AND DON'T JUDGE SO QUICKLY... UNTIL YOU HAVE LEARNED THE DESTINY YOU SET FOR YOUR FOLLY.

I RECALL LITTLE OF THE DAY I FIRST CAME INTO BEING.

THE STRANGE MULTITUDE OF SENSES RUSHED UPON ME FROM THE BLACKNESS, AND I FOUND MYSELF *TORMENTED* WITH LIFE.

I BEGAN TO SWIFTLY COMPREHEND MY LONELINESS, AND SO, FRIGHTENED AND HURTING, I FOLLOWED THE SOUNDS OF YOUR SOBBING.

5

*// //// -- ////
//// //// //// // //--
//-///-///*

YOU MAY HAVE SPOKEN, BUT I DIDN'T UNDERSTAND.

I ONLY KNEW THAT I WAS *ALONE* AGAIN.

BEWILDERED.

TERRIFIED.

KNOWING LITTLE OF WHAT TO DO WITH MYSELF, I VAINLY SOUGHT TO EMULATE YOU--DRESSING MY SHIVERING BODY IN YOUR CLOTHING AS BEST I COULD.

AT LENGTH, THE MENACE AND DESOLATION OF THE LABORATORY GREW TOO MUCH FOR MY AWAKENING SENSATIONS...THOUGH THE STREET OFFERED ONLY COLD AND STARVATION.

FINALLY, FINDING MYSELF TOO WEARY TO MOVE FURTHER, I SLUMPED DOWN AND BITTERLY WEPT UNTIL SLEEP OVERCAME ME.

THE END OF MY FIRST DAY.

TWEET TWEET TWEET

THE COMING OF THE BRIGHT MORNING STARTLED ME, FILLING ME WITH **WONDER**.

AND WAS NOT TO LAST.

IT WAS THE FIRST PEACE I HAD KNOWN.

EVERYTHING HAPPENED SO QUICKLY.

CHILDREN SHRIEKED. WOMEN FAINTED.

BEFORE LONG, THE WHOLE VILLAGE WAS ROUSED AND SET AGAINST ME.

SOME FLED AND OTHERS ATTACKED, HURLING ALL KINDS OF MISSILE WEAPONS, BRUISING ME GRIEVIOUSLY.

MY ONLY THOUGHTS WERE OF ESCAPE.

I ASSURE YOU THE ACTION I CONCEIVED WAS FOR MY OWN PRESERVATION.

HORRIFIED AND IN AGONY, I THREW MYSELF UPON THEM.

AT LENGTH, FEARING THE SHEER NUMBER OF THE MOB, I ESCAPED INTO THE OPEN COUNTRY.

FINALLY FREE OF THEIR ONSLAUGHT, THE OPPRESSIVE COLD CREATED A FURTHER HARDSHIP FOR ME.

FOOD WAS SCARCE...AND SHELTER WAS EXTREMELY DIFFICULT TO FIND.

GREAT SNOWFALL MADE MISERY OF THE FOREST IGH UNBEARABLE.

MY SITUATION WAS MUCH IMPROVED BY THE ADVANCE OF AN EARLY SPRING...

...WHICH GREATLY ALTERED THE ASPECT OF THE EARTH I'D COME TO KNOW.

WHAT WAS BEFORE MERE DESERT AND GLOOM NOW BURST FORTH IN THE DELIGHT OF A THOUSAND NEW SCENTS AND COLOURS.

AS ON JUST SUCH NSPIRED DAY THAT HANCE ENCOUNTER ERED MY LIFE.

FOREVER.

9

IT WAS... A *GIRL,* SWEET AND GENTLE OF NATURE, SOFTLY HUMMING, THINKING HERSELF ALONE.

MY SPIRIT LIFTED TO HER PINK AND PERFECT FORM.

I COULDN'T TAKE MY EYES AWAY.

TIMID, AND HURTING STILL FROM THE MOB, I DARED NOT REVEAL MYSELF, ALTHOUGH POWERFUL NEW EMOTIONS URGED ME TO REACH OUT TO HER.

TO TOUCH HER.

BEFORE I COULD GAIN MY NERVE, THE UNTIMELY APPROACH OF ANOTHER YOUNG CREATURE CAME TO DISTURB HER BATH.

IN ALL THERE WERE THREE COTTAGERS...

...A SILVER-HAIRED OLD GENTLEMAN--WHOM I LATER PERCEIVED TO BE BLIND--AND HIS CHILDREN.

I LONGED TO BE INSIDE WHERE THE GIRL PREPARED THEIR HOT SUPPER. I WANTED TO BE ONE OF THEM.

BUT, FOR ALL THEIR LOVE, THE YOUNG MAN SEEMED ALWAYS DISTANT AND SAD.

PERHAPS, ONE DAY, I WOULD TAKE MY PLACE AMONG THESE SIMPLE, GENTLE CREATURES.

ALTHOUGH I COULD SEE NO APPARENT CAUSE FOR HIS SORROW, I WAS GREAT-LY AFFECTED BY IT.

IF SUCH WONDERFUL BEINGS AS THEY WERE PRONE TO MISERY, IT SEEMED A COMFORT THAT I SHOULD BE SO WRETCHED.

ALMOST AT ONCE I RESOLVED TO RESIDE WITHIN A HOVEL ATTACHED TO THE COTTAGE.

LATER, I DISCOVERED BY MOVING A LOOSE BOARD THAT THE WHOLE ROOM WAS VISIBLE TO ME.

THE WEEKS PASSED HAPPILY FOR ME-- ONE WHO HAD NEVER WITNESSED KINDNESS BEFORE. I FELT PART OF THEM.

THE NEGLECTED WOOD SHED WAS INDEED A PARA-DISE COMPARED TO THE BLEAK FOREST.

I FELT HOME.

THE KINDLY FATHER, THE HARD-WORKING, MELAN-CHOLY SON, AND THE GIRL'S GRACE AND QUIET BEAUTY ALL ENTICED MY LOVE.

AFTER A SHORT WHILE IN THE HOVEL I SOUGHT TO SOOTHE THEIR BURDEN.

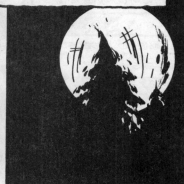

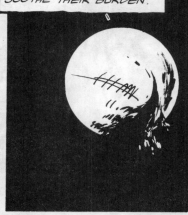

OWING WELL THAT MY E MADE ME MUCH STRONGER, I BEGAN NG UP THE YOUNG N'S CHORES AFTER HTFALL.

THE EASE OF THEIR DAILY DUTIES PROVIDED MY FRIENDS MORE LEISURE TIME TO SPEND TOGETHER, TALKING, READING AND SINGING TOGETHER--A SECRET PLEASURE I OBSERVED THROUGH THE CREVICE.

GIFTS THEY LEFT HEIR MYSTERIOUS PER FURTHER OURAGED MY FECTION.

D AND BLANKETS ED MY DISCOMFORTS, E THE USE OF THE KS, AT FIRST, LED ME GREATLY.

EVERY NIGHT, AFTER MY LABOURS, I PATIENTLY PRACTICED THE WORDS I'D HEARD DURING THE DAY.

FAM-I-LY ...LOVE...

AG-A-THA.

13

MOST OF THIS GOD-LIKE SCIENCE CAME EASILY, AS IF THE KNOWLEDGE LAY ALREADY IN MY BRAIN, DORMANT, AND NOW COMING TO LIFE.

I SOON CAME TO UNDERSTAND ALMOST EVERYTHING MY COTTAGERS SPOKE.

ONE MORNING I SOLVED EVEN ANOTHER MYSTERY...

SAFIE...?

...THE REASON FOR THE YOUNG MAN'S SORROW.

SAFIE! MY SWEET SAFIE!

THE VISION OF THEIR HAPPINESS HAUNTS ME STILL.

THE DAYS THAT FOLLOWED, I LEARNED THAT THE DE LACYS ARE POLITICAL EXILES, MADE TO LEAVE THEIR HOMELAND.

A WAR FORCED FELIX AND SAFIE APART. NOW THEY WERE TO BE MARRIED.

VERY GOOD, SAFIE. YOU'RE A QUICK STUDENT.

FELIX
LOVE
HUSBAND

AGATHA TUTORED HER IN THEIR LANGUAGE AS I LISTENED IN.

BEFORE LONG, I COULD FINALLY **READ** MY BOOKS.

EACH VOLUME PRODUCED NEW IMAGES AND IDEAS IN MY BRAIN, A NEVER-ENDING SOURCE OF ASTONISHMENT...

...RAISING ME TO ECSTASY...

...THEN SINKING TO THE **LOWEST** DEJECTION.

NOW I COULD READ THE PAPERS FOUND IN THE POCKET OF THE COAT I HAD TAKEN FROM YOUR LABORATORY.

IT WAS A JOURNAL OF FOUR MONTHS PRIOR TO MY... CREATION.

THERE WAS THE ENTIRE DETAIL OF MY **LOATHSOME** ORIGIN...

...CLIMAXED BY THE PROUD SIGNATURE OF MY "CREATOR."

VICTOR FRANKENSTEIN.

15

MY HOPES WERE CRUSHED. I WAS NEARLY INSANE WITH GRIEF AFTER THE HATEFUL DISCOVERY.

AND THERE WAS NONE TO WHOM I COULD SHARE THE PAIN.

AGATHA.

SHE WAS SO SOFT.

SO BEAUTIFUL.

I WANTED HER SO MUCH...

A MOTION ACROSS THE ROOM SUDDENLY STARTLED ME.

IT WAS HER DRESSING MIRROR.

I'D SEEN MY FIRST REFLECTION.

I HAD WANTED HER SO MUCH.

17

GREAT GOD!

WHAT ARE YOU??

I'LL NEVER FORGET AGATHA'S EYES WHEN, AT LAST, SHE SAW ME.

IT'S... IT'S A DAEMON!

GET BACK! GET AWAY FROM HIM!!

FELIX--NO! PLEASE...

NO!!

I WON'T BE BRUISED AGAIN!

UGHH--!

SOMEBODY --PLEASE! HELP US!!

AGATHA--?

AGATHA!

19

SHE HAD STRUGGLED JUST A MOMENT, THEN, AT LAST, I HELD HER CLOSE TO ME.

OOOOOOH...

MY POOR AGATHA.

I'M SORRY... SO SORRY...

BLAM

UNNNH...

FELIX--?

--STAY AY FROM R...I'M ARNING OU...

OH MY GOD.

ENOUGH-- DAMN YOU!

ENOUGH!!

SO--NOW EVEN YOU WANT TO KILL ME??

21

ONE AGAIN IN THE FOREST, REALIZED I WOULD NEVER INSPIRE LOVE...

...ONLY HATE AND HORROR.

MANKIND WAS MY BITTER ENEMY.

I VOWED REVENGE.

FOR ONCE, FATE SEEMED TO FOLLOW ME.

23

OHHH! WHO ARE YOU--?

YOUR *FRIEND*, I HOPE. ARE YOU HERE ALONE?

I'M NOT SUPPOSED TO BE THIS FAR INTO THE WOODS. JUSTINE WILL BE ANGRY.

I WON'T TELL HER.

YOU TALK *FUNNY*. WHERE DO YOU LIVE?

COME.

I'LL SHOW YOU.

I SWEAR, *FRANKENSTEIN*, THAT I MEANT NO HARM TO THE CHILD.

HE WAS NOT AFRAID OF ME, AT FIRST, AND I SOUGHT HIM ONLY AS A COMPANION TO MY LONELINESS.

NO! STOP!

LET ME DOWN--!

YOU PUT ME *DOWN!*

I'LL TELL MY *FATHER*-- THEN YOU'LL BE *SORRY!*

25

HUSH, LITTLE FRIEND --I WON'T HURT YOU.

YOU ARE HURTING ME! YOU'RE MEAN AND YOU'RE UGLY!

MY FATHER IS THE BARON FRANKENSTEIN-- AND HE WILL PUNISH YOU...!

FRANKENSTEIN!!

BARON...

...FRANKENSTEIN

HE WAS OF YOUR BLOOD.

A FITTING VICTIM... I KNEW HIS DEATH WOULD BRING YOU PAIN.

AT LAST...

...I STRUCK BACK AT YOU.

AFTER THE DEED I WAS SICK WITH REMORSE.

THE BOY HAD NEVER WRONGED ME...

...YET HE LAY *DEAD* BY MY HANDS.

LIKE THE LOWEST COWARD I CREPT UPON THE NAPPING GOVERNESS AND SLIPPED THE BLOODY LOCKET INTO HER CLOTHING.

TODAY THE INNOCENT GIRL WAS HANGED.

I AM *TWICE* A MURDERER-- *TWICE* A MONSTER!

YOUR MONSTER, FRANKENSTEIN.

AND THE CRIMES BEGAN THE NIGHT YOU *ABANDONED* ME.

YOU DARE BLAME ME FOR YOUR OWN *EVIL?*

ARE YOU SAYING THAT I SLAUGHTERED MY BROTHER... THAT I CONDEMNED JUSTINE TO THE GALLOWS??

I'VE HEARD ENOUGH!!

27

COME ON! COMPLETE YOUR REVENGE!

KILL ME--IF YOU WANT!

I WON'T STRUGGLE AGAINST YOU.

YOU HAVEN'T LISTENED. IT'S NOT YOUR DESTRUCTION I SEEK. I ASK YOU TO FINISH YOUR DUTIES.

YOU MUST CREATE FOR ME A FEMALE...A CREATURE AS DEFORMED AND AS HIDEOUS AS I.

A WOMAN--? NO...I COULD NEVER--

GOD, IN PITY, MADE HIS MAN AND WOMAN BEAUTIFUL --AFTER HIS OWN IMAGE. EVEN SATAN HAD HIS FELLOW DEVILS TO ADMIRE AND ENCOURAGE HIM.

I AM ALONE.

HAVE PITY ON ME, CREATOR.

GRANT MY PRAYER.

THIS ONLY YOU CAN DO.

YOUR...DEMAND IS MORE *COMPLEX* THAN YOU KNOW.

EN-- OU REE!

NOT NOW. I MUST HAVE TIME TO CONSIDER IT.

"TIME TO MOURN MY BROTHER."

ZABETH--!

OU ULDN'T E COME ERE ONE.

OH, VICTOR! I WAS SO AFRAID...

YOU DIDN'T COME HOME...I WAITED ...THEN I THOUGHT OF LITTLE WILLIAM--

SWEET COUSIN. I'LL NEVER LEAVE YOU AGAIN.

I PROMISE.

ET'S HOME, TOR.

PLEASE.

"I KNEW THE MONSTER WAS WATCHING.

"I KNEW WHAT HE WAS THINKING...

"...AS FROM THE HILLTOP HE REGARDED US WITH *ENVIOUS EYES.*"

"HE'S DYING, CAPTAIN."

"ARE YOU CERTAIN? THERE'S NO MISTAKE?"

"I'M SORRY, SIR. I CAN DO LITTLE MORE FOR HIM."

THE ICE IS BREAKING AND WE'LL BE FREE BY MORNING. PERHAPS I CAN BRING HIM TO A PROPER ENGLISH PORT AND--

MY DEAR FRANKENSTEIN, THE SHIP'S SURGEON TELLS ME YOU ARE MUCH IMPROVED.

DEAT HOLDS TERRO FOR M IS MO WELCO NOW

I ASSURE YOU THERE'S NO HOPE, CAPTAIN. IT'S BEST TO TELL HIM.

NONSENSE, CAPTAIN WALTON.

MY C REGRE FAILUR MIS

"...KNOWING THAT OUT THERE--

"--SOMEWHERE...

PERHAPS, VICTOR WILL LISTEN TO ME.

CLERVAL WILL BRING HIM AROUND. HIS FRIENDSHIP HAS ALWAYS BEEN *PRECIOUS* TO VICTOR. YOU DID RIGHT, CHILD, INVITING HIM HERE.

YOU'LL SEE.

VICTOR--*WAIT!* I MUST TALK TO YOU!

LET ME *BE,* HENRY. I DON'T WANT TO SEE YOU.

YOU MUST SPEAK TO *SOMEONE,* OLD FRIEND. YOU ARE TEARING YOUR FAMILY APART WITH YOUR SILENCE.

IT'S BEEN *MONTHS* SINCE WILLIAM'S FUNERAL. YOU'VE GOT TO FIND *PEACE,* VICTOR-- FOR *ALL* THEIR SAKES.

PEACE? THERE'S NO SUCH WORD FOR ME.

PLEASE COME BACK TO THE HOUSE WITH ME. WE WILL PUT THIS TRAGEDY BEHIND US--

I CAN'T. GO AWAY, HENRY.

JUST LET ME BE.

"HOW COULD ANYONE UNDERSTAND?

"I WAS GUILTY OF MY BROTHER'S DEATH AS IF I'D BEEN THE MURDERER MYSELF.

"HOW COULD I TELL HIM?

"AND ONLY ONE OTHER KNOWS THE AWFUL TRUTH."

Written by MARTIN POWELL Illustrated by PATRICK OLLIFFE Lettered by CLEM ROBINS Edited by CHRIS ULM

IT'S NO USE, ELIZABETH.

HE WOULDN'T LISTEN.

BUT WHERE IS HE GONE?

AWAY FROM US. AWAY FROM *HIMSELF.* WILLIAM'S DEATH *HAUNTS* HIM STILL.

VICTOR NEEDS TO GO AWAY, ELIZABETH. SOMEHOW--FOR HIS SAKE--WE MUST *MAKE* HIM LEAVE.

BEFORE IT'S *TOO LATE.*

IT'S BEEN *MONTHS,* FRANKENSTEIN. I WANT YOUR ANSWER.

I KNOW WHAT YOU EXPECT. YOU THINK I'LL REFUSE, AND THEN YOU WILL WREAK VENGEANCE UPON THE REST OF MY FAMILY--THE REST OF *HUMANITY.*

YOUR THIRST FOR *VIOLENCE* BETRAYS YOUR TRUE MOTIVES.

YOU ARE WRONG.

I'VE REASONED WITH YOU RATHER THAN THREATENED. LET ME INSPIRE *LOVE* INSTEAD OF FEAR AND HATRED.

THE LOWEST BEAST HAS A MATE TO CLING TO AND CHERISH --AM *I* NOT WORTHY OF THIS?

I SWEAR BY THE HOPE IN MY HEART, IF YOU ANSWER MY PRAYER, NONE SHALL EVER LOOK UPON US AGAIN.

SHE WILL JOIN ME TO THE WILDS OF SOUTH AMERICA AND WE WILL BE TOGETHER AND HAPPY, GROWING OLD IN OUR LOVE...

HOW WOULD YOU LIVE? YOU WOULD BE *OUTCASTS,* WRETCHED AND UNEARTHLY TO HUMAN EYES. CAN I BE CERTAIN THE FEMALE WOULD NOT JOIN YOU IN REVENGE AND MURDER?

...AND IN MY LAST, DYING MOMENTS, I WILL NOT *CURSE* THE MEMORY OF MY CREATOR.

PLEASE.

"I WAS MOVED.

"I HAD DELIBERATED MANY WEEKS ON HIS REQUEST, SHUDDERING WITH THE TERRIBLE POSSIBILITIES.

"YET THE CREATURE WAS PROVING HIMSELF A BEING OF DEEP FEELINGS AND ELOQUENCE...

"...AND WAS NOT I, HIS CREATOR, RESPONSIBLE FOR THOSE SENSATIONS?

OWE HIM, AT LEAST, A CHANCE OF HAPPINESS?"

ENOUGH.

I'VE DECIDED.

I WILL DELIVER INTO YOUR HANDS A FEMALE.

"AND SO, I WAS BOUND FOR ENGLAND.

"CLERVAL HAD INSISTED ON JOINING ME."

THERE, VICTOR! THAT'S THE PLACE!

"THE FIEND WOULD FOLLOW ME, I KNEW. I SOUGHT TO LEAD HIM AS FAR FROM MY FAMILY AS POSSIBLE.

WHAT'S WRONG? IF YOU'D PREFER A DIFFERENT INN--

I'M SORRY, HENRY. I MUST BREAK OUR ALLIANCE AND TRAVEL ON WITHOUT YOU.

PLEASE TRUST ME, MY FRIEND. I NEED SOLITUDE NOW. I WILL RETURN FOR YOU.

THEN I WILL WAIT, VICTOR. GODSPEED.

"HOWEVER EXCELLENT WERE MY MOTIVES, IT WAS DIFFICULT LEAVING CLERVAL BEHIND.

"I HAD COME TO DEPEND ON HIS WARMTH AND QUIET STRENGTH. NEEDLESS TO SAY, MY COMPANIONSHIP THREATENED HIS VERY LIFE. I COULDN'T TAKE SUCH A RISK.

"ONCE ALONE, IT WAS LIKE A REVOLVING NIGHTMARE...

"ONCE AGAIN I HAUNTED THE CARNAL HOUSES.

"ONCE AGAIN MY FOOTSTEPS ECHOED WITHIN THE HOLLOW VAULTS.

"THE HORROR HAD BEGUN.

"THROUGH NO CHOICE OF MY OWN.

"...THERE COULD BE NO TURNING BACK.

"I SELECTED A RUINED FORTRESS ATOP A LONELY SCOTTISH ISLE, TO BEGIN THE FILTHY PROCESS.

"THUS, COLLECTING THE GRIM INSTRUMENTS OF MY GOAL, I RETIRED FAR FROM UNWANTED EYES...

"...FINDING SOME SMALL SOLACE IN THE ISOLATION...

"...AND HARDENED MYSELF TO THE MORBID WORK.

"THE MONTHS PASSED-- A BLUR OF BODY-SNATCHING AND MIDNIGHT SURGERY.

"I THOUGHT OFTEN OF ELIZABETH.

"SOON, IT WAS OCTOBER ONCE MORE."

"FINALLY EMERGING FROM THE AWFUL TOIL, A GHASTLY REFLECTION HAD COME TO ME.

"NOT LONG PAST, I'D CREATED IN THE SAME MANNER A MURDERING DEVIL SUCH AS THE WORLD HAD NEVER SEEN.

"NOW, I WAS COMPOUNDING THE EVIL, FORMING YET ANOTHER SUCH MONSTER...

ND HOW WAS I TO FORETELL NATURE OF THIS BEAST?

"SHE MAY BECOME A THOUSAND TIMES MORE TERRIBLE THAN HER MATE...

"THEY COULD CONCEIVABLY PROPAGATE A RACE OF DAEMONS, SET FROM BIRTH TO BE THE ENEMY OF MAN.

NO!!

I WON'T DO THIS!

"I WAS MAD TO AGREE WITH THIS TERRIBLE PLAN.

"I DARED NOT FINISH.

HE MAY KILL ME--BUT I WILL NEVER DO THIS THING!

NEVER!

"THE FEMALE WOULD NOT LIVE.

"MY CONSCIENCE RUSHED UPON ME, AWAKENING MY TRUE LOYALTIES...

"...AND I ENDED OUR UNHOLY CONTRACT."

NO...

LIAR!

SO THIS IS HO YOU KE YOUR WORD

YOU'VE HAD YOUR CHANCE FOR FREEDOM! MARK ME WELL...

I WILL BE WITH YOU ON YOUR WEDDING NIGHT!

LEAVE ME... FRANKENSTEIN...

GET OUT!!

AAAAAAAH!

REVENGE.

"THE HOWLING TEMPEST MERCIFULLY DROWNED THE SCREAMS OF THE FIEND, AS I TOOK FLIGHT INTO THE WIND AND THE WAVES.

"DELIRIUM HAD DULLED MY BRAIN, AND NIGHTMARES FLUTTERED HORRIBLY BEHIND MY EYELIDS.

"WHEN MORNING FINALLY CAME I FOUND MYSELF ASHORE.

Y MIND CLEARED OWLY, AND I AKLY GROPED R A PLAN TO OTECT MYSELF.

"I SOUGHT CLERVAL.

Traveler's INN

"I REALIZED MY SECRETS FROM HIM HAD BEEN FOOLISH.

"I WOULD NOW TELL CLERVAL EVERYTHING ...OF THE MONSTER, THE MURDERS...

"HENRY CLERVAL LOVED ME, WAS DEVOTED TO ME. TOGETHER WE WOULD BRING THE MONSTER DOWN."

HENRY--?

THERE 'E IS, OFFICER! THA'S THE MAN--THEY WAS TRAVELLIN' TOGETHER...

..'IS NAME'S FRANK'STEIN!

WHAT'S HAPPENED HERE? WHERE IS HENRY CLERVAL?

HE'S HERE, M'LAD.

NOW THEN--WHERE'VE YOU BEEN?

GOD.

"IT HAD STARTED ALREADY...THE DEVIL'S REVENGE.

HENRY

"COWARDLY, I LET THE MADNESS SWEEP OVER ME."

YOU'VE A VISITOR, FRANKENSTEIN.

GO...GO AWAY...

HE'S BEEN IN THIS STATE FOR *MONTHS*, BARON FRANKENSTEIN. THERE'S LITTLE WE CAN DO, HE SEEMS TO HAVE GIVEN UP.

VICTOR, MY SON...WE MUST LEAVE THIS TERRIBLE PLACE. YOU DON'T BELONG HERE. EVERYONE KNOWS YOU'RE INNOCENT OF YOUNG CLERVAL'S MURDER.

NO, I *AM* GUILTY, FATHER. I WANT TO *DIE*...

WE'VE COME TO TAKE YOU HOME.

VICTOR, PLEASE--DON'T SPEAK LIKE THAT.

ELIZABETH...?

ELIZABETH! MY DEAR GOD!

IS IT *REALLY* YOU...?

IS IT...

IN THE FACE OF GOD AND THESE WITNESSES --I PRONOUNCE YOU MAN AND WIFE.

"UNDER ELIZABETH'S SWEET AND TENDER CARE, I SOON RECOVERED, AND FORGOT MY GUILT.

"IN CELEBRATION OF MY RETURN TO LIFE, WE WERE MARRIED THE FOLLOWING SUMMER IN MY FATHER'S CHAPEL.

"IT WAS THE CONSUMATION OF A CHILDHOOD DREAM.

VICTOR, I'M SO HAPPY.

"ALTHOUGH I THOUGHT NO MORE OF MONSTERS, I DIDN'T FEEL FREE."

I'VE NEVER SEEN YOUR FATHER SO GIDDY, VICTO. I HOPE WE DIDN'T LEAVE TOO EARLY.

VICTOR--?

DEAREST, WHAT'S THE MATTER? AREN'T YOU COMING TO BED?

NO...NOT JUST YET. I WANT TO MAKE CERTAIN THE CABIN IS SECURE. I'LL ONLY BE A MOMENT.

NO ONE WILL DISTURB US HERE, VICTOR...

21

DON'T GO.

STAY WITH ME.

"SHE WAS SO LOVELY.

"WE HAD WAITED SO LONG..."

WHAT WAS *THAT*?

SOMEBODY'S OUT THERE--!

VICTOR...?

A...A *NOISE*, DEAREST. OUTSIDE THE CABIN.

SURELY YOU HEARD IT?

IT'S PROBABLY NOTHING...A RABBIT OR A FOX. THAT'S ALL.

COME BACK TO ME.

THAT WAS NO *ANIMAL*.

VICTOR--*PLEASE* COME AWAY FROM THE WINDOW. THERE'S NO ONE OUT THERE.

I KNOW.

I NEED TO MAKE SURE. ONLY FOR A MOMENT...JUST TO BE *SAFE*.

YOU'RE SCARING ME VICTOR...

DON'T LEAVE ME --IF YOU LOVE ME...

PLEASE...

I'LL LOCK THE DOOR AND TAKE THE KEY WITH ME. DON'T BE AFRAID. IT'S PROBABLY *NOTHING* ...LIKE YOU SAID.

VICTOR--? PLEASE *DON'T!*

VICTOR!!

CLICK!

23

I FELT SICK FOR LEAVING HER.

I HATED MYSELF FOR THE TERROR IN HER EYES.

"HOW COULD I HAVE EXPLAINED THAT I'D SUDDENLY SENSED THE LOATHSOME PRESENCE OF MY CREATURE...?

"WITH PISTOL READY, I WAITED HIS COMING.

"HIS BURNING, HATEFUL PROMISE BOOMED IN MY BRAIN...

"'I WILL BE WITH YOU ON YOUR WEDDING NIGHT'.

"BUT THERE WERE ONLY FIREFLIES IN THE WOODS."

I SAW NOTHING, MY DEAR. PROBABLY JUST A RABBIT.

ELIZABETH? ARE YOU ASLEEP ALREADY?

ELIZABETH...?

4

"TO MY HORROR A SINGLE WINDOW GAPED OPEN."

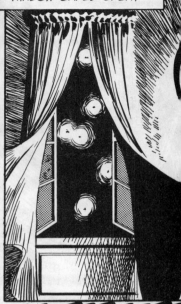

ELIZABETH...NOT ELIZABETH...

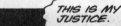

THIS IS MY JUSTICE.

NOW WE ARE *BOTH* ALONE.

YOU *MURDERER*

I'LL KILL YOU--!

DO YOU LIKE THE *PAIN*, FRANKENSTEIN? YOU HAVEN'T *BEGUN* TO SUFFER!

OUR *DUEL* IS NOT OVER!

I SEEK THE FROZEN WASTES OF THE ARCTIC. FOLLOW ME, CREATOR.

I MUST *SEE* HIM.

TO *KNOW* THAT HE IS DEAD.

FRANKENSTEIN...

IN YOUR *MURDER* MY CRIMES ARE COMPLETE.

WHAT...WHAT GOOD IS IT NOW TO ASK YOUR *FORGIVENESS*?

IT IS ENDED. YOU ARE MY *LAST* VICTIM.

WRETCH! *MONSTER*!!

YOUR *REPENTANCE* COMES *TOO LATE*! IT'S YOURSELF THAT YOU PITY--NOW THAT NATURE HAS ROBBED YOU OF YOUR *REVENGE*!

YOU ARE *WRONG*.

DO YOU THINK THE DEATH *GROANS* OF HIS WOMAN *PLEASED* ME? WICKED AS I AM, THE ACT OFFERED NO PLEASURE ...NO *PEACE*.

MAN OVERBOARD!!

CAPTAIN-- WHO IS IT? SHOULD WE ATTEMPT A RESCUE?

"NO.

"HE IS...A *MONSTER*. DRIVEN BY HATE AND TORN BY BITTER REMORSE.

"AND IN MANY WAYS... A VICTIM HIMSELF.

"THE ICE IS *BREAKING*. THERE'S NOTHING WE CAN DO.

"SOON HE WILL BE BORNE AWAY BY THE WAVES...

"...AND LOST IN THE DARKNESS AND DISTANCE."

• GRAPHIC NOVELS •

ABBOTT & COSTELLO
The crazy comedy duo is back in this classic collection of the misadventures from the 40s and '50s.

CHINA SEA
An epic adventure in the tradition of Terry and the Pirates.

DINOSAURS FOR HIRE
Three gun-crazy Dinosaurs on the loose as private eyes!

FU MANCHU
Sax Rohmer's villainous creation stars in two classic adventures.

NINJA HIGH SCHOOL
One boy, two girls, giant robots. Trouble ahead.

PERRY MASON
The world's most famous lawyer stars in four classic cases.

PLAN 9 FROM OUTER SPACE
The only authorized adaptation of the worst movie ever made!

SCARLET IN GASLIGHT
An all new epic adventure pitting the world's greatest detective against Cound Dracula!

SCIMIDAR
The adventures of a female bounty hunter in the year 2005. Contains nudity and sexual situations.

SHERLOCK HOLMES
The world's greatest detective is featured in 6 full length adventures from the newspaper strip of the '50s.

SPICY DETECTIVE STORIES
Illustrated fiction from the naughty pulps of the '30s and '40s.

SPICY TALES
Uncensored comics from the pulps of the '30s.

TEEN ANGST
A treasury of pre-code '50s romance stories.

THREE STOOGES
Nyuk! Nyuk! Nyuk! The Knuckleheads return in collection of their looney antics.

THREE MUSKETEERS
All for one and one for all in this new adaptation of the classic Dumas novel.

TIGER-X
In the late 20th Century, a Soviet invasion has split the U.S. in two.

TROUBLE WITH GIRLS
Lester Girls longs for the quiet life, if only the fabulous babes, ninja assassins, and relentless reporter Maxi Scoops could leave him alone.

WAR OF THE WORLDS
The Aliens Have Landed! Based on the H.G. Wells novel.

Don't cut up your comics! A photocopy of this coupon is acceptable!

ABBOTT & COSTELLO___$17.00 * CHINA SEA___$7.00

NINJA HIGH SCHOOL___$9.00 * TIGER-X___$10.00

DINOSAURS FOR HIRE Guns N' Lizards___$7.00 * Dinosaurs Rule!___$7.00

FU MANCHU___$14.00 * PERRY MASON___$18.00 • PLAN 9___$6.00

SCARLET IN GASLIGHT___$8.00 • SCIMIDAR___$11.00

SHERLOCK HOLMES___$20.00 • SPICY TALES___$11.00

SPICY DETECTIVE STORIES___$8.00 • TEEN ANGST___$15.00

THREE STOOGES___$17.00 * THREE MUSKETEERS___$11.00

TROUBLE WITH GIRLS (Vol. One)___$9.00 • MY NAME IS GIRLS (Vol. Two)___$9.00

WAR OF THE WORLDS___$11.00

I certify that I am over 18 (required for Scimidar)

Signature_____

Name (please print)_____

Address_____

City_____ State_____ Zip_____

Minimum order: $10.00 All prices include postage (US orders only--Canada and Mexico add $1.00 per order. Overseas add $3.00 per order). Please allow 4-6 weeks for delivery. Do not send cash. Make money orders and checks payable to Malibu Graphics, Inc., 1355 Lawrence Drive #212, Newbury Park, CA 91320. Please list alternates.

SCIMIDAR

BOOK III • ALL NEW STORY & ART

Created & Written by R.A. Jones
Illustrated by Rob Davis

FOR ADULTS ONLY
FROM ETERNITY COMICS

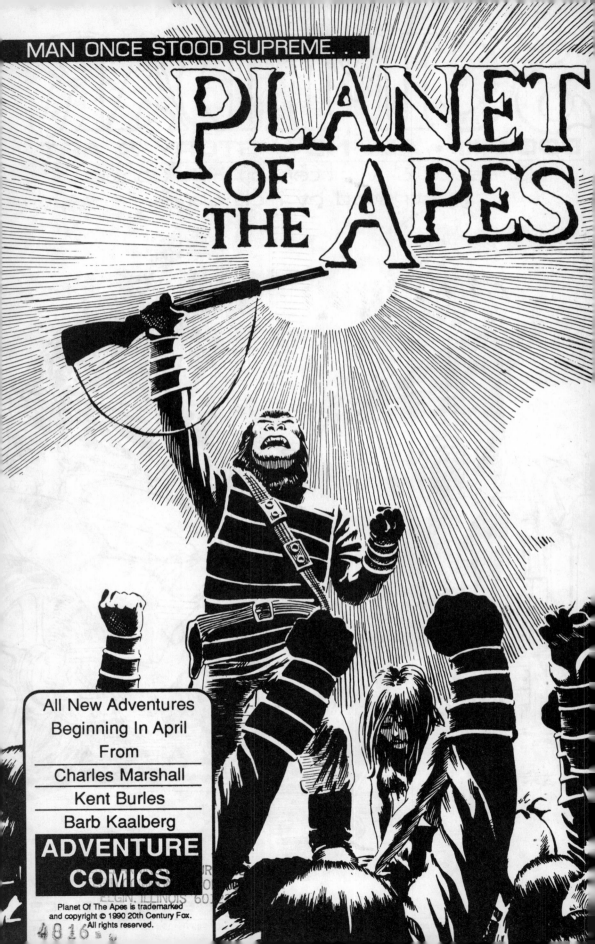

MAN ONCE STOOD SUPREME...

PLANET OF THE APES

All New Adventures
Beginning In April
From
Charles Marshall
Kent Burles
Barb Kaalberg
ADVENTURE COMICS

THE LEGEND RETOLD

Mary Shelley's classic novel of science gone mad brought to life in this critically acclaimed adaptation by Martin Powell and Patrick Olliffe. Obsessed with his own mortality, young Victor Von Frankenstein discovers a means to imbue dead tissue with life. In fit of pride, he creates an unnatura monster from fresh corpses and sets events in motion which will cost the gifted doctor his loved ones, his sanity and ultimately, his life

HORROR
ISBN # 0-944735-39-8
$9.95 • $11.95 in Canada